25th Anniversary Edition

Yellow Ball
Molly Bang

Purple House Press
Kentucky

With thanks to Mr. Schuman
and his third grade class
for helping me learn
to draw BIG,
to Grant Langford,
and to Monika.

Pastels and some tempera were used for the full-color art.
The text type is 42 point Folio Medium.

Published by Purple House Press
PO Box 787, Cynthiana, KY 41031
Copyright © 1991 by Molly Bang. All rights reserved.
ISBN: 978-1-930900-79-0   LCCN: 2015948030

Summary: During a beach game, a yellow ball is accidentally
tossed out to sea, has adventures and finds a new home.

Find more classic books for kids at
www.purplehousepress.com

Printed in South Korea by PACOM
1 2 3 4 5 6 7 8 9 10
First Edition

To David

Catch

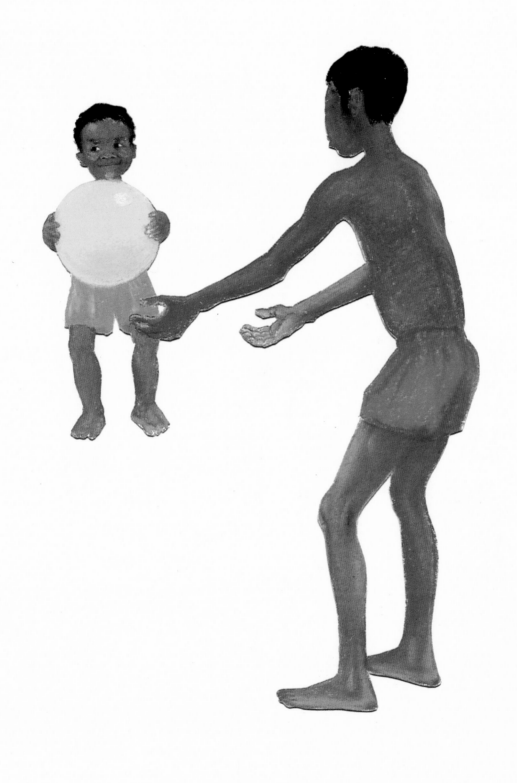

Throw

Uh-oh

Too late now

The sea is so big

High   Low

Above

Below

Wind blowing

Storm growing

Watch out!

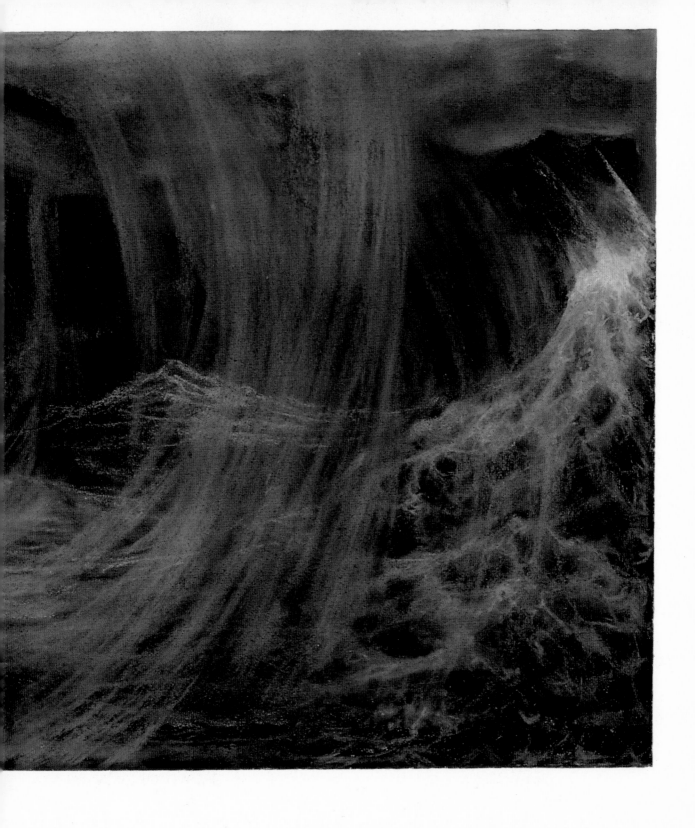

Quiet now

Coming ashore

Look

Hug

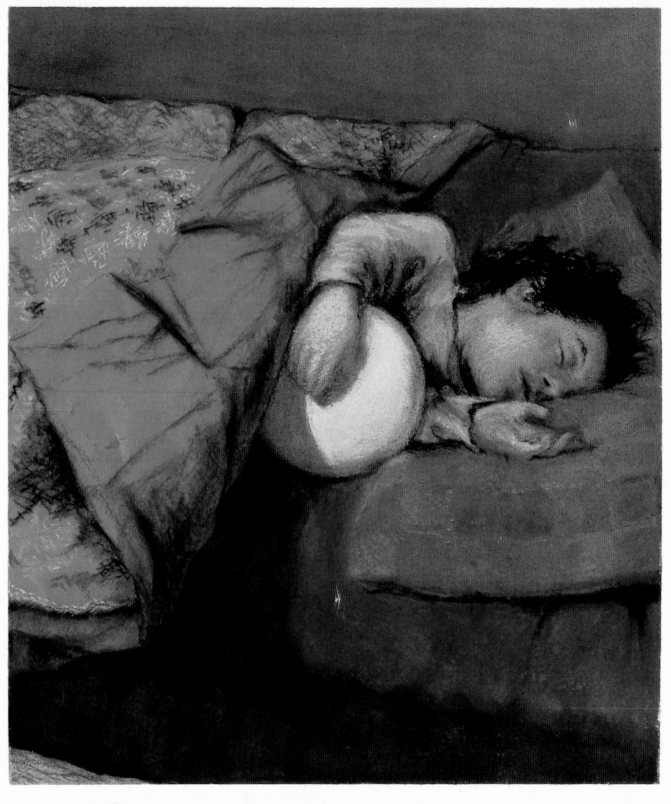

Home